Paul Bunyan
vs.
Hals Halson

The Giant Lumberjack Challenge!

Teresa Bateman   Illustrated by **C. B. Canga**

Albert Whitman & Company, Chicago, Illinois

For Tori, Dani, Lisa, Julene, Carrie, and Steve, who've bravely taken the big step of joining the family.—T.B.

To my children, Rocky, Trinity, and Emma.
Thank you for teaching me the meaning of love, and for inspiring me to be my best.—C.B.C.

Library of Congress Cataloging-in-Publication Data

Bateman, Teresa.
Paul Bunyan vs. Hals Halson : the giant lumberjack challenge! / Teresa Bateman ; illustrated by C. B. Canga.
p. cm.
Summary: Hals Halson, who is nearly as tall as the legendary Paul Bunyan, strides into a logging camp determined to prove himself the greatest lumberjack in North America, despite Paul's attempts at friendship.
ISBN 978-0-8075-6367-0
1. Bunyan, Paul (Legendary character)—Juvenile fiction. [1. Bunyan, Paul (Legendary character)—Fiction. 2. Competition (Psychology)—Fiction. 3. Loggers—Fiction. 4. Tall tales.] I. Canga, C. B., ill. II. Title. III. Title: Paul Bunyan versus Hals Halson.
PZ7.B294435Pau 2011 [E]—dc22 2010025881

The design is by Carol Gildar.

For more information about Albert Whitman & Company, please visit our web site at www.albertwhitman.com.

There are as many tales told about Paul Bunyan as stars in the sky, and most of the stories are just as hard to grab hold of.

Sure, Paul was big, but as a baby he was no bigger than your average grizzly bear despite what folks say.

And fast? Yes. But he didn't outrun the North Wind.
It was clearly a tie.

The point is you can't believe everything you hear about Paul. Here's the truth.

He was born big, and growing six inches a day as a boy, he just kept getting bigger.

By the time he was old enough for school, Paul was too tall to fit inside. He had to watch through the window, squinting to see the blackboard.

Paul didn't have many friends growing up. It took everyone in the school to balance the teeter-totter with him on it, and he couldn't play tag or hide-and-seek. He was too fast to catch and too big to hide.

He was so big he had to watch out for those smaller than himself, so fast he had to work to be slow, and so strong he had to learn to be gentle.

Sometimes it was hard not having someone his own size around.

In those days great forests covered the country. Folks wanted land cleared for crops, and lumber for cabins and wagons. Needing more elbow room than most, Paul decided to become a lumberjack. He was hard-working and earned a good reputation for both chopping down trees and making sure there were plenty left to grow. Folks clamored for his services, but few invited him to dinner.

If it weren't for his pet, Babe, he would have spent a lot of time alone. Babe was a giant ox—bright blue and big enough to match Paul step for step. He was a wonder, but let's leave that story for another day. Babe filled some of the holes in Paul's life, but the lumberjack was still lonely.

One day Paul was sitting
in lumber camp when the
ground began to shake.
BOOM swish BOOM
swish BOOM swish.

Into camp strode a giant of a man who was nearly as tall as Paul himself! But when Paul reached out for a friendly shake the stranger snarled, "I'm Hals Halson, and I've come to prove who's the greatest lumberjack in North America. When I beat the tar out of you we can settle the issue once and for all."

Paul was puzzled. "There's no need to fight," he replied. "Think of the work that needs doing. Together we could make a terrific team. Instead of knocking each other down, shouldn't we be knocking these trees down together?"

Hals Halson didn't answer. He just charged, grabbing Paul in a wrestling hold.

"That tickles," Paul laughed, "and could you scratch just below my left shoulder? I've got an itch there that's been bothering me for the last month."

Hals roared, released Paul,
then kicked the friendly
lumberjack in the shins.
"Well, shucks," Paul said.
"That's a waste of a good pair
of boots."

Poor Hals Halson was hopping around, the toe of his boot bent straight up.

Furious, he tried tossing Paul over his shoulder, but might as well have tried uprooting a redwood. "Soon as you're done we can sit down and have a chat," Paul said. "Sourdough Sam will have fresh biscuits out of the oven shortly."

"Shorty?" howled Hals Halson. "Are you saying I'm SHORT?"

SOURDOUGH SAM'S
KITCHEN

He backed up half a mile, scraped his feet on the ground like an angry bull, then charged towards Paul.

When Hals's head hit Paul's stomach, there was a sound like a gong. All the trees for five miles lost their leaves, and loggers came running thinking it was the dinner bell.

Hals reeled back, twirled twice, then dropped like a rock at Paul's feet.

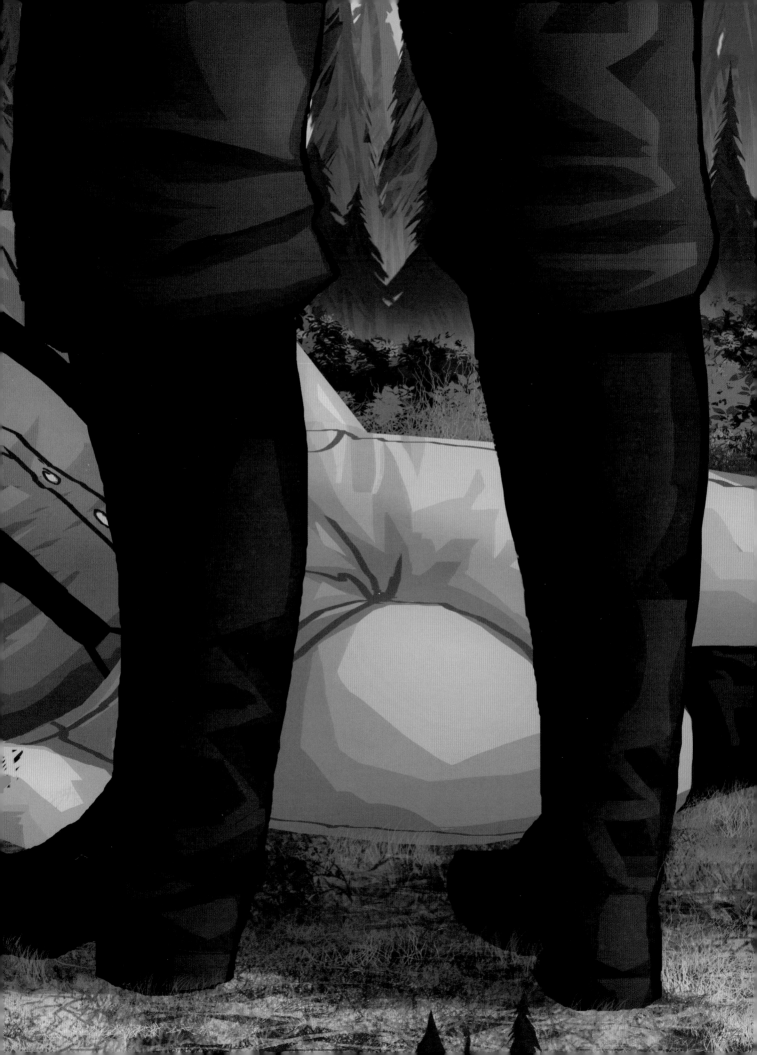

Paul rubbed his stomach a moment. "Hey, let's be careful or one of us might get hurt."

He leaned back and waited an hour or two. Finally Hals opened his eyes. Paul helped him to his feet and handed him some fresh biscuits.

Hals groaned as he stood up. "How'd you like to hire the SECOND-best lumberjack in North America?" he asked.

Paul smiled and shook his hand. "Welcome to camp," he said. "I think we'll be good friends."

And from that day on they were.

Stories about Paul Bunyan have been around for more than 150 years. No one is quite sure where they began, but it's certain he was North American from the toe of his logging boot on up . . . and up . . . and up. Paul and his companion, Babe the Blue Ox, were talked about in logging camps on the East Coast. As folks moved west, so did Paul.

The tales grew wilder and more fantastic as the years went by until there were frying pans you could skate on, mosquitoes big enough to carry off houses, and rumors that Paul was responsible for the Grand Canyon itself. Paul Bunyan "tall tales" are always stretched to the limit and show off not just his strength and size but also his cleverness, good-heartedness, and sense of humor. That's why they were always welcome around the cookstove of any logging camp and became a part of American folklore.